MALARKEY BOOKS
PO BOX 331
ASBURY MO 64832

SIC IS
VER!

or The Facts Concerning the
Disappearance of Juntaro Yamanouchi

BEN ARZATE

MALARKEY BOOKS

Cover design by Mark Wilson
Typeset by Michael Kazepis

Published by Malarkey Books, 2022.
Malarkeybooks.com

Print ISBN: 978-1-0880-1534-6

Dedicated to Darrell Jurmu (1941-2019)

"In its essence, any art that relies on words makes use of their ability to eat away--of their corrosive function--just as etching depends on the corrosive power of nitric acid."
--Yukio Mishima, SUN AND STEEL

"Fuck compose. Fuck melody.
Dedicated to no one. Thanks to
no one. ART IS OVER."
--Juntaro Yamanouchi

"The passion for destruction is a creative passion, too!"
--Mikhail Bakunin, THE REACTION IN GERMANY

THE GEROGERIGEGEGE!

ONE TWO THREE FOUR!

MUSIC IS OVER!

ONE TWO THREE FOUR!

Juntaro fixed his makeup in the mirror. In the bed of the love hotel room, the chubby salaryman that he'd come with had fallen asleep. He didn't mind. It wasn't a satisfying encounter, but he couldn't remember having one since Tetsuya died. He put his makeup back in his purse and stared at his reflection for a moment. He wondered how much longer he'd be able to stave off the inevitable signs of aging that would eventually come.

Juntaro walked out of the bathroom. He looked over the salaryman's naked body sprawled out on the bed. In the past, the image may have stirred him to wake up his partner for tonight by sucking his cock. Tonight, however, it only made him want to go home and be alone. He grabbed his hat off the floor, put on his shoes, and left the room.

As he passed the front desk he felt self-conscious in his blouse and skirt. He held his breath until he got outside onto the sidewalk. There used to be a thrill in coming to these love hotels that prohibited gay male couples. He was almost always able to pass himself as a woman without the staff suspecting a thing. Knowing that he might be found out made his visits with Tetsuya or some other man he picked up even more exciting. Now it didn't seem worth it. He regretted not just having the salaryman take him to one that catered to gay men.

He started his walk home, the neon lights of the Shinjuku district burning above him. The cool night air and the sounds of the city cleared his head and he soon realized that his stomach was rumbling. He found the nearest convenience store and bought some snacks. He brought them to a bench just a couple blocks away and sat down to enjoy them.

As he ate his egg sandwich, he heard footsteps approaching. He glanced up to see a woman walking toward him with her head down. He figured she must be drunk or tired and went back to eating. He felt the bench shake slightly as the woman sat down quickly on the other side as if her legs had given out. He looked over at her. She was rummaging in her trench coat pocket for something. He noticed she was wearing a surgical mask. It wouldn't have bothered him, but he also noticed a wide scar running down her cheek and behind the mask. He remembered hearing the rumors, but he thought that they couldn't be true. They were just ghost stories.

Then the woman slowly turned her head toward him. Her gaze made him freeze. She leaned toward him with her eyes wide and said, "Am I pretty?"

Juntaro's mind scrambled for the right thing to say, but nothing came out of his mouth. The only thought that came clearly to him was that if his bowels weren't empty, he would have evacuated them right there.

ONE TWO THREE FOUR!

The woman laughed as Juntaro sat frozen in fear on the bench. She reached up and pulled down her surgical mask. To his relief, her mouth wasn't slit open. Two wide scars extended from the ends of her lips forming a Glasgow smile and indicating that it might have been at some point, but she clearly wasn't who he thought she was. Juntaro breathed a sigh of relief and laughed with the woman.

"Let me guess," the woman said, "you thought I was Kuchisake-onna, didn't you?"

Juntaro nodded.

"You scared the hell out of me."

"You aren't the first. I freak people out all the time when I'm out at night. It's annoying sometimes, but it keeps the drunk men from bothering me."

"I don't know why I got so scared. I usually don't fall for ghost stories."

"Oh, no. It's no ghost story," she said as she pointed to her face. "How do you think I got this?"

Juntaro laughed again.

"Come on, stop messing with me," he said.

"I'm not. I'm serious."

"Come on, you can't be."

"I wouldn't joke about that. I was scared to death when she stopped me. I don't know how I didn't faint when she showed me that horrible mouth. I'm just lucky I answered her questions right."

"It doesn't look like you did."

"If I answered them wrong, I'd be dead. I tried telling her she was average, like the rumors said, but when I tried to get away, she appeared in front of me again asking if she was pretty. I said yes that time. It hurt so bad when she cut my mouth, but it was better than her taking my head. I'm lucky I was close to a hospital."

"That's awful!"

"It's made things harder. I was never that interested in dating, so it didn't bother me that men stopped hitting on me. But everyone at work started avoiding me and stopped inviting me to after-work drinking. They only ever talk to me when they need to for work. My friends never call me anymore either. They make excuses when I try to call them to hang out. Even my family hardly ever bothers with me now."

"Are they afraid you're cursed?"

"That might be part of it. I think they just don't like how I look now. Even other women don't have time for a woman with no beauty."

"Well, for what it's worth, I think you still look pretty."

"Thank you."

The woman stood up and bowed.

"I'm very sorry to spill all this on a stranger. My name is Kotono."

Juntaro stood up and bowed back.

"No, no. I'm sorry for being scared by you. My name is Jun. It's nice to meet you."

Juntaro figured it was better to give her his gender-neutral name. It was always easier to give strangers that when he was crossdressing than to explain he was actually a man.

"I'm so sorry, but can you help me with something else?" Kotono said.

"Of course, what is it?"

"I don't come to Shinjuku very often and I can't find my way back to the station. I want to get there before the last train leaves. Can you tell me where it is?"

"Sure. I can lead you there."

"I wouldn't want to trouble you."

"It's no trouble at all. Follow me."

Kotono pulled her mask back on. Juntaro picked up the plastic bag with his snacks and began leading her toward the Eidan station.

ONE TWO THREE FOUR!

"So where do you live?" Juntaro said to Kotono.

"Edogawa."

"That's pretty far. What brought you to Shinjuku?"

"Boredom, to be honest. I had a good time with my friends when I came here before, so I decided to come back."

"Did you enjoy yourself?"

"About as much as I usually do when I go out. I just ate dinner at a nice restaurant and found a bar to drink in for a while. It was the same as any other time I go out. I tried to figure out something else to do here since I came all this way, but I couldn't. Have you ever had that happen? The things that you used to enjoy just became a routine?"

Juntaro thought about the salaryman's naked body.

"Yeah. I know what you're talking about," he said.

"I felt like I was stuck just doing the same things day in and day out. I thought maybe a change of scenery would break me out of it. I just don't know what will."

Juntaro looked up at the sky. The lights of the city were too bright to see any stars. He could see, however, that the moon was a crescent like a mocking smile on its side.

"I've had a similar problem," he said. "I'm a musician. Or maybe I was. I've been trying to make something new, but I just can't. I try to start something and I just can't finish it. None of it sounds right."

"Oh. What kind of music did you make?"

Juntaro thought for a moment.

"Mostly punk rock," he said.

"What instrument did you play? Or were you a singer?"

"I kind of did everything and brought other musicians in to help when I needed. I had another member in my band. He was also kind of my, uh, my boyfriend. He died recently. I think that's why I can't work anymore."

"I'm so sorry! That must have been hard."

"I've just felt lost since then. I just can't get started."

"I hope you can again. I used to really want to be a poet. I even won a prize at my college for my writing. But after I got a job at an insurance company, I just stopped. I don't even know why. Now I'm just stuck in my daily routine with no idea how to get out. Sometimes I feel like those subway trains; stuck on the rails and just going back and forth where I need to every day."

"Oh, yeah. The station is just up here."

ONE TWO THREE FOUR!

The station was quiet and nearly empty as they walked in. Juntaro was used to being at the station while it was bustling during the day with people rushing in and out to get to their trains on time. The quiet and emptiness struck Juntaro as unsettling. Kotono pulled her phone out of her pocket and flipped it open.

"Oh no," she said. "It's just after one. I really hope I'm not too late."

Juntaro heard footsteps and it nearly made him jump. He realized how on edge he was as he took a deep breath. An Eidan worker came toward them from one of the ticket gates. The name tag on his uniform read "Genzo."

"Are you two looking to catch the train?" he said to Juntaro and Kotono as he approached them. "Afraid you're too late. Last one just left."

"Oh no! Now what do I do?" Kotono said.

"I guess you'll need to catch a cab," Genzo said.

"I'm going out to Edogawa. That's going to be expensive."

Genzo looked down one of the passageways.

"Well," he said, "I might be able to help."

"Really?" Kotono said.

"You see, there's a new night train that Eidan's been testing. It's only been used by employees so far, and it's my turn to ride it tonight. It won't take you all the way to Edogawa, but it will get you a lot closer."

"I haven't heard of that," Juntaro said.

"It's been kept a secret. If people knew about it, they'd be trying to get on. I'm not supposed to be telling anyone, so don't spread it around. It might get me fired," Genzo said.

"I don't know," Kotono said. "I don't want to get you fired or anything."

"Don't worry about that," Genzo said. "It's only going to be me and the conductor, and the conductor isn't going to see you in the passenger car."

"Well, all right."

"Okay. Follow me. I'll lead you to it."

Genzo started walking down the passageway, his footsteps echoing in the empty station.

"That sounds really suspicious," Juntaro said to Kotono.

"It does, but I'm kind of curious to see what he's talking about," she said

"I have to admit that I am too."

"I hate to ask this, but can you come with me? I'd rather have someone with me just in case."

Juntaro nodded. "If this turns out to be some kind of trick, we'll run away. Let's try to keep a little distance to be safe."

Juntaro and Kotono started following Genzo down the passageway. As they walked, Juntaro looked around, still on edge. Genzo led them past an open ticket gate and farther into the station. He brought them to a door labeled "For Staff Only" and led them inside. As they descended a staircase, Juntaro found himself getting more and more nervous. The sight of security cameras on the ceiling was somewhat comforting. There was no way Genzo would try anything when he could easily be seen. He thought about telling Kotono they should turn around and leave when Genzo brought them to yet another door, realizing he couldn't figure out where they were in relation to the rest of the building. Kotono went inside before he could say anything and he decided he needed to stay with his new friend.

ONE TWO THREE FOUR!

The platform that Genzo brought them to looked disused. There was a musty smell hanging in the air. The chairs and gates were made of wood, some of which looked partially rotted. The hanging signs were difficult to read through the layers of dust covering them. The train, on the other hand, was impeccable, despite looking like it was from the 1930's. It had a bright copper color and the bolts that held it together were visible. It looked very little like the sleek, white trains that Juntaro was used to riding.

"Sorry about how messy it is," Genzo said. "The platform is going to be renovated before this opens to the public."

"I hope that train is going to be replaced, too," Juntaro said. "That thing looks ancient."

"It's actually one of the first trains made for the subway. It's being used to test this night route for now. We're going to replace it with a new one when we open this route."

Juntaro and Konoto looked at each other. Juntaro wasn't sure he believed Genzo, and he could tell by the look on Kotono's face that she felt the same.

The doors on the train opened. Genzo boarded and motioned for the two to come on.

"I don't know, Kotono," Juntaro whispered to Kotono. "I don't like this at all."

"This is pretty weird," she whispered back. "Maybe we should turn back."

"Are you two coming?" Genzo said. "We're leaving in just a moment."

"Are you sure this train is safe?" Kotono said.

"Safe as any other train. Probably even safer since we're the only ones riding."

Konoto reluctantly stepped forward, looking back at Juntaro as if she wanted to be assured he was going with her. Juntaro followed her and both of them got on the train.

The interior made stepping inside feel like stepping seventy years into the past. The brown interior, the design of the seat cushions, and even the lighting fixtures were all straight out of a pre-WWII Japan. Yet it looked brand new, the only indication of its age being the faded signs advertising products with outdated logos, many of which weren't even sold anymore.

"You two go ahead and have a seat," Genzo said. "I need to go talk to the conductor. I'll come get you when we reach the destination. Enjoy the ride!"

Genzo bowed and walked through the door to the next car, heading toward the front of the train.

Juntaro and Konoto sat next to each other. Juntaro was surprised at how cozy the seat was.

"This is even more comfortable than the seats on the newer trains," he said.

"I think it looks better, too," Kotono said. "I wish they still made trains like this."

"They probably wouldn't be as fast as the new ones."

"I think that's a problem with everything today. Too many people care more about everything getting done fast. We don't take enough time to stop and look around at things."

The train started moving. It moved more smoothly and quietly than Juntaro expected it to.

"I thought this would be more rickety, as old as it is," he said.

"I thought so, too. It's like it was built to last instead of being rushed out cheaply and quickly. There are too many things made like that. It isn't just things we use like trains or clothes or phones. I feel like I can't turn on the TV or listen to the radio without seeing a show or listening to a song that I know I'm going to forget as soon as it's over."

"Man, I know what you mean."

Juntaro looked through the window. The lights of the subway tunnel formed a solid strip surrounded by blackness.

"My mom played piano and taught me it, so I grew up around music. Everyone I knew at school just listened to pop music that I couldn't hear any lasting appeal in. I never took music seriously because of that. I thought you could only play in an orchestra like mom or make dull pop for the radio. Then a friend of mine gave me a Ramones record. It was fun, but so raw and full of emotion. It showed me what you could really do with music."

"The Ramones. They're the ones who did 'The Blitzkrieg Bop' aren't they?"

"That's their most famous song, yeah."

"Sorry, I don't listen to much rock. Mostly just classical music."

"Ever hear of Jani Christou?"

"I don't think I have."

"I came across a tape of some of his compositions and it impacted me as much as The Ramones did. I was playing in punk bands for a while, but it didn't really go anywhere. Listening to Jani Christou inspired me to go out and try my own thing. I had a lot more success with that."

"I'll have to find some of his music. It was my parents that got me into classical. They mostly listened to Western music. I think

Steve Reich was the first I heard that really caught my ear. Have you listened to him?"

They continued talking about classical music, their conversation carrying them through the long subway tunnel.

ONE TWO THREE FOUR!

Juntaro took out a green tea Kit Kat from his bag of snacks and shared it with Kotono as they waited for their stop. She took her phone out of her pocket and flipped it open. She looked at the time.

"We've been riding this thing for half an hour without stopping," she said. "We have to be close to wherever the stop is."

"We haven't left the tunnel either," Juntaro said. "It's weird a route this long would be entirely inside."

"Genzo hasn't come back either. I'm starting to get worried."

"Maybe we should go find him."

"What if he's still with the conductor? I don't want him to get in trouble or anything."

Juntaro put the bag of snacks in his purse and stood up.

"Let's just try to find him," he said. "If we don't see him before we get to the conductor's car, we'll just hang back. We should find out where this is dropping us off at least."

Kotono stood up. She walked by Juntaro as they walked to the next car.

"Oh, yeah!" Kotono said. "I'm so sorry. I didn't even think about how you're going to get home. You live back in Shinjuku, don't you?"

"I do. Don't worry. I'll find a hotel by the station and ride back tomorrow."

"You can spend the night at my place. It's small, but I have an extra futon."

"I wouldn't want to impose."

"It's no problem at all. It's the least I could do for staying with me, especially when you met me just tonight."

"I don't know. It just seems like we have a lot in common. Maybe it's just that we're both lonely and miserable."

Kotono laughed.

"How does that Western cliché go?" she said. *"Misery loves company?"*

Juntaro laughed with Kotono.

"Too bad you're not a man," Kotono said. "I might actually be interested for a change."

Juntaro let out a nervous chuckle. He knew he'd have to tell her the truth at some point but now didn't seem like an appropriate time.

He looked around as they entered another car. Unlike the prior two, which looked like they had been cleaned just hours before they arrived, this one looked like it hadn't had anyone inside in some time. There was a layer of dust on the floors and on the seats. Juntaro felt the dust they kicked up as they walked tickle his nose. He sneezed.

"Take care, Jun," Kotono said.

"Excuse me."

Kotono giggled.

"You think someone is talking about you?" she said.

"I doubt it. It's all this dust. Look at it, it's way dirtier than the car we were sitting in."

"It really is now that you mention it. Did the person cleaning the train get lazy?"

"Maybe they were expecting Genzo to stay in the last two."

When they walked into the next car, it was even dirtier and more dilapidated. The dust was thicker and the seats had holes in them. Some of the hand rails were broken off and lying on the ground with other pieces of garbage and broken glass from the windows. Juntaro and Kotono had to step over them as they walked through the car. Several of the lights were out and a couple flickered.

"Okay, what's going on?" Kotono said. "Why would they put a car in this condition on this train?"

"The cars are just getting worse. Genzo wasn't telling us the truth. I knew it."

"I thought so, too. I should have just gotten a cab."

"Well, we're here now. I say we keep going and see what we can find."

Kotono nodded. Juntaro approached the door to the next car. He opened it and saw that the next car was pitch black.

"I don't think we should go in there," Kotono said.

"I don't want to go in there either, but where else do we go?"

"We could go back and wait for the train to stop."

"I'm pretty sure that's what Genzo wants us to do and I don't trust him. How about this, we'll do Janken. If I win, we go in that car. If you win, we go back and wait."

Kotono nodded. She and Juntaro raised their fists. Before they had a chance to even begin chanting, their decision was made for them. A loud grinding indicated the brakes had been activated. Juntaro and Kotono braced themselves against the wall, surprised at how fast the train stopped. When it came to a complete halt, the doors creaked open as if it was the first time they'd opened in years.

Juntaro and Kotono approached the nearest door to the outside. It was too dark to see much, but they could tell they were at another subway platform.

"We'd better get going before Genzo comes looking for us," Juntaro said.

"I think so too. I don't know where we are, but I'd rather take my chances out there."

Juntaro and Kotono stepped onto the platform. It smelled even mustier than the one where they boarded the train. Juntaro tried looking around, but it was too dark to see anything beyond where the light from the train poured out. Kotono reached into her pocket and pulled out her phone. She flipped it open. The light from the screen wasn't strong, but allowed them to see right in front of them.

"Good idea, Kotono!" Juntaro said. "Let's find our way out of here."

Kotono shined the screen around. The platform was nothing but bare concrete as far as they could see. While they walked away from the train, they couldn't see any benches, signs, or columns. Finally, they came to a staircase. They climbed up and came to a wooden door. Juntaro looked back and hoped Genzo wasn't following them before he pushed the door open.

31

ONE TWO THREE FOUR!

Juntaro and Kotono walked through the doorway into a cavernous room. It resembled a warehouse that no one had used in years. It was like the bigger version of the subway car they had just left. Debris littered the floor. A light musty smell filled the air. A large doorway was open on the other side. Juntaro looked around and saw that pieces of ceiling were broken out. He was surprised he could see the stars and the moon through the holes. It took him a moment to realize that the moon was full. He wondered if he should point that out to Kotono but then decided he shouldn't disturb her any more than she likely already was.

"This doesn't look like a station. Where are we?" Kotono said.

"I have no idea. Let's get outside and find a street sign."

The two walked across the room and out through the large doorway. Outside, Juntaro could tell they were in some sort of industrial area. They had walked out of what was indeed a warehouse and into a large lot. There were faint sounds of cars and machinery all around. Rather than the skyscrapers of Shinjuku he was familiar with, smoke stacks, buildings that resembled factories, and silos extended toward the sky. Smoke billowed up from some of the stacks. Elevated walkways were lit up and he could occasionally see the outline of someone on them. He wasn't sure if he should be relieved to see people or worried about who was there.

"Where the hell are we? Are we even still in Tokyo?" Kotono said, sounding even more scared than she was on the train.

"It looks like it took us to one of the industrial zones outside of Tokyo."

"How can that be? There's no way we were on the train long enough. How are we going to get back?"

Juntaro pointed to the open phone that Kotono was still holding in her hand.

"Let's do what we should have done and just call a taxi. It'll be more expensive, but it'll get us back."

Kotono looked at the screen of her phone.

"I don't know the number," she said. "I don't have one saved. I rarely use them."

Juntaro looked around again.

"We'll try to find someone who can tell us," he said. "It looks like some of these factories are still running so one of them has to have a phone book."

Kotono nodded. They walked across the lot toward the fence that surrounded the lot where it opened to the street. Juntaro looked to the left and saw a small building on the other side of the street. Despite the industrial buildings around it, its signs clearly indicated that it was a bar called Goodnight Work 36. He pointed it out to Kotono.

"That's a strange location for a bar," she said.

"It looks like it's open. Let's see if someone there can help."

They crossed the street. Just as they got to the other side, a truck went speeding by. They both jumped as the driver honked the horn and screamed something that Juntaro couldn't understand except for the word "ass." He watched the taillights of the truck disappear down the road. He felt himself shaking. He hadn't even realized how on edge he still was. He looked over and could see Kotono was on the verge of crying.

"You might want to take that mask off," he said. "I think it's better that people are wary of us while we're here."

Kotono nodded. She took off her surgical mask and tucked it in her pocket. They walked toward the bar. Juntaro kept looking up the road and hoped no more headlights came toward them.

ONE TWO THREE FOUR!

The bar looked like any other dive that Juntaro had been to in Tokyo. The kind he went to when he just wanted a quiet place to have a couple drinks alone and not meet any men. Thinking back, he regretted not just going to one tonight instead of the usual club he went to for hookups. It was empty except for two men in gray jumpsuits and hard hats sitting at a table in the far corner in silence. Neither of them looked up as Juntaro and Kotono approached the bar.

The bartender was a skinny bald man with a face that didn't give away his age. He looked up at Juntaro and smiled.

"Well, hello there!" the bartender said. "What can I get for you, er, you two?"

The bartender hesitated and his smile dropped when he saw Kotono's scarred face.

"I'm sorry, but we're actually lost and we need a taxi to take us home," she said. "Do you know the number for one?"

"There are no cabs here," the bartender said. His tone was much colder. "Especially not at this hour."

"Can you tell us where we are?" Juntaro said.

"You're in my bar."

Juntaro looked at Kotono, who shrugged.

"Are we close to Tokyo?" Juntaro said. "We're trying to get to Edogawa."

"Look, lady, are you buying drinks or not?"

"If we buy some will you help us out?"

"Sure, sure."

"Okay, I'll have an Asahi Super Dry."

"I'll take that, too," Kotono said.

The bartender poured two beers and placed them in front of his two clearly unwelcome guests.

"1,000 Yen," he said.

Juntaro got the money out of his purse and put it on the bar. The bartender picked up the money, walked over to the cash register, and put the money in. He walked to the middle of the bar and started washing glasses.

"So are you going to tell us where we are?" Juntaro said.

The bartender lifted his head, gave an annoyed look at Juntaro, and went back to washing glasses.

"You said you'd help us if we bought drinks!" Kotono said, raising her voice.

"Shut up or I'll throw you both out!" the bartender yelled.

The two men looked up from their table briefly before going back to staring at their drinks, occasionally taking a sip but never making any noise.

Juntaro put his hand on Kotono's shoulder.

"Forget that asshole," he said quietly to her. "He's obviously not going to help."

The two took their beers over to a table. Kotono sat down.

"I'm going to go ask those two over there," Juntaro said.

He walked over to the two silent men.

"Excuse me," he said as he bowed to them. "I'm very sorry to interrupt you, but can you tell me where this is? My friend and I are lost."

The two men looked at Juntaro. They didn't say anything as they stared at him with expressionless faces. Juntaro felt very uncomfortable.

"I'm so sorry," he said as he bowed again. "I'm sorry to have bothered you."

As he walked back to the table where Kotono was, the two went back to staring at their drinks. He sat across from her and took a sip of his beer.

"The people here aren't very friendly," Juntaro said.

"No kidding. Now what do we do?"

"I guess since we're here we may as well finish our drinks."

Kotono nodded and took a drink of her beer.

Juntaro heard someone else come through the door of the bar and turned to look. He was surprised to see that it was a foreigner. He was used to seeing them in Tokyo, but he rarely saw them whenever he was outside the city. He realized it was a reassuring sight. If a foreigner could find their way here, he and Kotono would be able to find a way out. He may even be able to give them directions.

The foreigner was an odd-looking man wearing a bright red polo shirt and baggy jeans. His hair was styled into a pompadour with so much gel that it almost looked plastic. He smiled at Juntaro and Kotono when he saw them looking at him. He walked to the bar and ordered a Sapporo Yebisu in Japanese with a fluency that impressed Juntaro. He was used to hearing foreigners speak brokenly or very slowly to avoid stumbling over their words.

The foreigner walked over to the table where Juntaro and Kotono were sitting. He grabbed a chair from the table next to theirs and sat down with them.

"Do you beautiful girls mind if I join you?" he said.

Juntaro grinned and nodded. He thought the foreigner was a handsome man in spite of his ridiculous Bōsōzoku hair. Kotono seemed less pleased and mumbled that it was fine.

"My name is Keith, and may I ask yours?"

"I'm Jun, and this is my friend Kotono," Juntaro said as he bowed. Kotono bowed slightly to acknowledge his introduction.

The foreigner put his hands together and did an exaggerated bow in his seat.

"Pleased to meet you both. My name is Keith," he said.

Juntaro giggled.

"You speak Japanese very well," he said.

"Well, I had to learn it so I could speak with all the pretty girls in this country."

Kotono rolled her eyes and took a drink of her beer.

"You don't need to be cold," Keith said to her. "I'm a very nice man, even if I am American."

Juntaro laughed again. He found Keith to be very charming. He thought it was too bad that he was probably straight. Kotono clearly didn't feel the same. She sat there stone-faced, drinking her beer.

"What brings you to Japan, Keith?" Juntaro said.

"I'm trying to find a friend of mine," Keith said. "See, he's a doctor and came here to practice. But then I lost all contact with him. I couldn't call him, couldn't email him, couldn't even find an address. He just disappeared. So I'm going to every place that he's been seen to try to find him."

"I'm so sorry to hear that! I hope you find him soon."

"We wouldn't want to get in your way," Kotono said.

"Don't worry about that!" Keith said. "I always have time for drinks with beautiful girls."

"You're too kind," Juntaro said, giggling.

"Are you ladies from around here?" Keith said.

"Actually, no. We stopped here because we're lost."

"Oh no!"

"Yeah, we asked the bartender for help, but he was just very rude to us."

Keith turned around and looked at the bartender. He was wiping the bar down and seemed to be trying to ignore everyone else as best as he could.

"I'll have to have a talk with him later," Keith said. "I can't abide being rude to the ladies."

"You're very kind, Keith. Thank you so much," Junataro said. "You wouldn't happen to know how to get to Tokyo from here, would you?"

"Afraid I don't. I just go where I hear that my friend has been spotted. I haven't even been to Tokyo yet."

"Well, I hope you do visit. It's a great place. Kotono and I can't get back there fast enough."

Kotono sat as the two chatted, sipping on her beer and saying nothing. She and Juntaro jumped in their seats when a police siren started up nearby. Even Keith seemed to tense up. He went quiet until the sirens went by and the sound faded out.

"Are you okay?" Juntaro said to Keith.

"Oh, yeah, I'm fine!" Keith said. He took a big gulp of his beer. "I just need to get going. My friend isn't going to find himself!"

"Oh, okay."

Keith took another big gulp of his beer and got up. On his way out, he pointed to the bartender.

"Hey, you, barkeep!" he said. "You be nice to your customers, especially ones as pretty as them!"

The bartender looked up at Keith and gave him a dirty look. He raised his middle finger at Keith.

"*Fucking asshole*," Keith said in English before he walked out the door.

Kotono sighed.

"Sorry about that," she said. "I get really uncomfortable around foreign men. Some have harassed me very badly before. They think they can do whatever they want to Japanese women."

"No, I understand," Juntaro said. "I've had experiences like that before too. He seemed okay, though."

"I don't know. Did you see how weird he acted when he heard that police siren? He must have been up to something."

"You have a point. That was very suspicious."

Juntaro didn't notice the two men at the other table had gotten up and were also walking out. One of them reached into his pocket, pulled out a piece of paper folded into an origami crane, and tossed it in front of Kotono as he passed their table. Before she or Juntaro had a chance to say anything, both were out the door.

Kotono held the crane up, admiring how well-constructed it was.

"Wait, it looks like there's writing on it," Kotono said.

"Unfold it. Maybe it will help us out."

"Well, I hate to undo it. It's really nice. I hope it is useful."

Kotono unfolded the origami crane. She read the paper and then handed it to Juntaro. At the top it read "This Will Help You," and gave directions on how to get from the bar to what it simply said was a "building." Though it didn't say what the building was or what was there that would help them.

"It looks suspicious to me," Kotono said.

"It does to me too," Juntaro said. "The way they looked at me earlier didn't exactly say they were in any mood to do anything for us."

"Should we just ignore it?"

"Well, we don't have anywhere else to go. We may as well see where this takes us."

"I agree. It's better than just sitting here."

Juntaro and Kotono finished their beers. They got up and headed out the door. As they were walking away, Juntaro stopped and looked back at the bar.

"Is something wrong?" Kotono said.

"No. Just give me a second."

Juntaro walked back to the bar, opened the door, and poked his head inside. The bartender was picking up their glasses from the table.

"Hey!" Juntaro yelled.

The bartender looked up at Juntaro, his face scrunched in anger.

"Your beer tastes like shit!"

Juntaro slammed the door and jogged back to Kotono laughing. Kotono smiled and laughed with him as they walked up the side of the road.

ONE TWO THREE FOUR!

As Juntaro and Kotono walked on the side of the road they kept looking behind them and to their sides. Their time in the bar hadn't exactly put them at ease with this place. They passed by factories, warehouses, and the occasional office building. Once in a while, a car or truck would go speeding by, heading one way or the other. Juntaro would tense up when one was coming, but nobody in them yelled or honked their horn.

They didn't come across anyone else as they walked—the lack of a real sidewalk made it seem as if walking was discouraged here—except for a man who appeared to be homeless. He wore a jacket that was too heavy for the season and his jeans had holes in the knees. He was filthy all over. His oily hair hung down to his shoulders, over one of which he carried a bag that was just as dirty as the rest of him. Kotono kept her head down, hoping he wouldn't say anything to them. He gave them a quick glance. Juntaro met his gaze but he just walked past them. Kotono gagged as his body odor hit her. He smelled like a rendering plant. Juntaro, however, had smelled worse things.

After they'd been walking for a while, they came to a bus stop. The sign gave no information other than informing that it was, indeed, a bus stop. It didn't even give the name of the local transit service. The blue paint on the metal bench was peeling in several places and it was covered in scratches.

"Let's take a rest here," Kotono said. "It's even farther than I thought it was going to be."

Juntaro nodded. They sat down. He pulled the directions from his purse and read them over again.

"It says we need to keep going this way until we get to an intersection and take a left," Juntaro said. "I think we're going the right way, or maybe these directions really are bullshit."

"I hope not."

"We've got to hit something if we keep going this way. Even if we hit the outskirts of wherever we are, we might find some signs to direct us."

"That's good thinking. I haven't seen any . . ."

Before Kotono could finish, another police siren started blaring. Juntaro looked down the road and saw the police car with its red lights flashing. He hoped that they were just passing by. Then he noticed the car was slowing down. His fears were confirmed when the driver started speaking on the PA over the siren.

"You two!" the policeman's distorted voice said. "Stay there! Get up slowly with your hands in the air!"

Juntaro and Kotono followed the instructions. The car stopped and the two policemen got out of the car with their guns drawn. The one coming out of the driver's seat was an older, heavyset man with his brows furrowed in anger. His partner, coming around the other side of the police car, was much thinner and younger. His face looked as if he was barely out of his teenage years and his uncertain expression exacerbated that.

"Get on the ground slowly and put your hands behind your back! Now!" the heavyset policeman said.

Juntaro and Kotono did as the policeman told them.

"What is this about?" Kotono said as the younger policeman handcuffed her.

"The owner of the bar down the street was just murdered," he said.

"That's impossible," Juntaro said. "We just came from there."

"Exactly," the heavyset policeman said as he lifted Juntaro back to his feet with his hands cuffed behind his back. "So guess who the prime suspects are?"

The policemen threw their two detainees in the back seat of their car and drove off.

ONE TWO THREE FOUR!

The heavyset policeman pushed Juntaro into the interrogation room. It was bare but for a table with two chairs on opposite sides with a small trash can next to it, a single light on the ceiling, and a filing cabinet in the corner. The other, younger policeman had pulled Kotono into another room. Juntaro felt disoriented. This had happened so fast. One moment he was just walking with Kotono and the next he was arrested for murder. The policeman patted him down.

"No weapons on you, right, girly?" he said.

Juntaro shook his head. The policeman felt around his chest.

"Kind of flat, aren't you?"

Juntaro was starting to panic in his mind. Especially when the policeman's hands wandered down to his thighs and his ass. He hoped the policeman would be satisfied with groping him there. He had no way of knowing how he would react if he found out he was really a man.

Thankfully, the policeman stopped and pulled Juntaro's purse from around his shoulders. He dumped the contents on the floor. He looked down at the contents, pushing the makeup, wallet, and pieces of paper around with his foot.

"Looks like you're clean," the policeman said. "Have a seat."

The policeman pulled Juntaro to the table. He forced him on to the chair, his hands still cuffed behind his back. The policeman walked a slow lap around Juntaro, staring intently down at him before he took a seat at the other side of the table. Juntaro was sweating, wishing more than ever before that he was back home.

"So," the policeman said, "are you going to tell us how and why you killed the bartender, or are we going to have to do this the hard way?"

"I didn't kill him!" Juntaro said. "Neither did my friend! He was alive when we left!"

"We have a witness. Just confess and you might just avoid getting hanged."

Juntaro's stomach dropped.

"A witness?" he said.

"The bartender's wife was in the back. She heard someone telling him that his beer tasted like shit. Then, just a little bit later, she heard a struggle and then someone running. She came out and found her husband dead on the floor. He was stabbed over seventeen times. Seventeen times. That was kind of excessive, don't you think? Especially since you just didn't like his beer?"

"I didn't do it! I did tell him his beer tasted like shit, but I didn't stab him! I left right after that!"

"So, girly, why don't you tell me your side of things?"

Juntaro explained everything from how they came to the bar looking for help, how the bartender was rude, the two men at the other table, the foreigner, and the directions on paper they were given.

The policeman snickered. He got up and walked around the table to Juntaro.

"Now, now, girly," the policeman said. "Do you really expect me to believe that fucking bullshit!"

The policeman's sudden shouting made Juntaro instantly jump and tense up. He leaned into Juntaro, his hot breath blowing in his face as he berated him.

"Do you know what's going to happen to you? They're going to take this pretty neck and they're going to put it in a noose!"

The policeman wrapped his hand around Juntaro's neck.

"It'd be a shame to see a pretty little piece of ass like you die. But you're a murderer and you deserve it. I bet you'll look pretty even when you're standing on that trap door. I love seeing girls like you with fear in your eyes. It gets me so fucking hard."

The policeman's voice was getting low and breathy. Juntaro could see nothing but prurience in his eyes. He was frightened on the one hand, but, on the other, he couldn't deny that the situation and the policeman's aggressive dirty talk was starting to turn him on.

"Please," Juntaro said in a seductive whisper. "I didn't do it. Please let me go. I'll do anything."

He hoped he could convince the policeman to take a blowjob from him in exchange for releasing them both. It wasn't a foolproof plan, but one that made a lot of sense in Juntaro's mostly scared, somewhat horny mind.

"Are you trying to bribe an officer?" the policeman said.

He started running his hands over Juntaro's chest again, feeling his nipples through his blouse.

"You are hiding a weapon, aren't you?" the policeman said. "You have it hidden down here, don't you?"

The policeman ran his hands down Juntaro's body to his legs. He started pulling up his skirt, reaching under and feeling up his thighs. His hands moved up toward his crotch.

"No, no!" Juntaro said.

He recalled a story that he'd heard several years ago. Another crossdresser he knew in Shinjuku had gone to a love hotel with a drunk salaryman who was unaware that he wasn't a woman. In his inebriated frustration, the salaryman beat him so badly, he gave him two black eyes and a broken nose. Gay-bashing was incredibly rare in Japan, so hearing about the incident had shocked him. He could only guess what this less-than-stable cop was going to do.

The policeman's hands ran over Juntaro's panties. His cock was hard from the fear and excitement. He was certain the policeman was about to lose his temper as he saw the confusion on his face.

"What have you got hiding in here?" he said. "Have you been trying to fool an officer, girly?"

"Look, I can explain," Juntaro said.

"What's there to explain? That you're a pervert?"

The policeman started squeezing Juntaro's cock through his panties.

"I think you need to be punished for being a naughty little pervert."

To his surprise, the policeman seemed to have an even more lecherous look in his eyes than before. He knew this just might be the way to get Kotono and himself out of this situation.

"Please, sir," he said. "Punish me. I deserve it."

The policeman brought his face close to Juntaro's.

"That's right," the policeman said, breathing heavily. "I'm a police officer. You will refer to me as 'sir.' A citizen like you is dirt under my feet. I'm going to make you pay for your crimes."

The policeman pressed his lips against Juntaro's, kissing him deep and hungrily. Juntaro moaned into his kiss, feeling him roughly grope the hard-on under his skirt. He grabbed Juntaro around the waist and pulled him up out of the chair. He reached to his side and pulled his baton out of his belt.

"Turn around and kneel. Now," the policeman said.

Juntaro obeyed the policeman. He pressed the baton against his cheek and stroked it with the weapon. For a moment, Juntaro was worried the policeman was going to crack him across the head. Instead, the policeman bent down, kissing his neck and whispering in his ear.

"Did you kill the bartender?" the policeman said.

"No, sir. I swear I didn't," he said.

"Did you try fooling a police officer into thinking you were a pretty girl?"

"I did, sir. I'm so sorry, sir. Please forgive me."

"Oh, no. You don't get off that easily. You need to be punished."

The policeman grabbed Juntaro's head and slowly brought it to the floor, keeping his other hand on Juntaro's hip so his ass was in the air. He pulled Juntaro's skirt up, exposing his panties. The policeman grabbed Juntaro's panties by the waistline and tore them off with one quick pull. Juntaro let out a surprised yelp.

The policeman stuck his baton between Juntaro's leg. He rubbed it against his balls and hard cock. Juntaro let out a soft moan of pleasure. The policeman brought the baton up the crack of Juntaro's ass and across it, gently massaging it before bringing the baton up and swinging it hard against him. Juntaro cried out in a mixture of pain and pleasure.

"Oh, god!" Juntaro said. "Punish me more, sir! I deserve it!"

The policeman brought the baton against Juntaro's ass again and again.

"You naughty little pervert!" the policeman said. "How dare you dress up and try to trick and seduce me!"

"I'm sorry, sir! I'm so sorry!"

By the time the policeman was done, Juntaro's ass was bright red and his cock was twitching and leaking precum. The policeman was breathing heavily from his exertion and, from what Juntaro could assume by the bulge in his pants, being incredibly turned on. The policeman unzipped, letting his hard cock out.

"Are you going to fuck me, sir?" Juntaro said. "Please fuck me, sir. I need it so badly. I'm . . ."

The policeman cut off Juntaro's begging by bringing the baton across his ass yet again.

"How dare you beg for that?" the policeman said. "I only fuck women. Not disgusting perverts like you that pretend to be women."

"I'm sorry, sir!"

"This is what you get instead."

The policeman walked over to the filing cabinet and opened one of the drawers. Juntaro could turn his head enough to see him reach in and pull out a bottle of lubricant. He knew that this wasn't the first time this cop had done something like this.

The policeman squeezed some of the lubricant on the end of his baton. He walked back over to Juntaro, moving his gloved hand between rubbing the lube all over the baton and masturbating. He spread Juntaro's ass and slowly slid the end of the baton into his anus. Juntaro shivered as he felt it going inside him.

The policeman fucked Juntaro with his baton while he jerked off. Juntaro moaned, his cock twitching as the baton rubbed against his prostate.

"You like this?' the policeman said, jerking off faster. "You're an even bigger pervert than I thought!"

"I am, sir! It feels so good!"

"You criminal! You pervert! Fuck!"

The policeman groaned and shot his cum on Juntaro's ass. The mixture of the baton in his ass, the policeman's insults, and the warm semen hitting him was too much. He cried out and came as well, his jism shooting on the interrogation room floor.

The room went silent but for Juntaro and the policeman panting with exhaustion. The policeman tossed his baton aside, grabbed Juntaro by his hair, and lifted his head off the floor. He put Juntaro's ear to his mouth.

"Here's the deal, girly," he said. "I'll let you and your friend go on one condition. What just happened never leaves this room."

Juntaro nodded.

"Okay, I promise," he said. "I won't tell anyone."

"You'd better not. If my wife ever finds out about this . . ."

The cop took his gun out of its holster and held it to Juntaro's temple. Junatro whimpered quietly and closed his eyes.

"Then the next time anyone sees you or your fucking friend will be in the river with bullets in your heads. Understand?"

Juntaro nodded again. The policeman re-holstered his gun.

"Then we have a deal, girly," he said.

He removed the handcuffs from Juntaro. Juntaro's arms fell to his side and he breathed a sigh of relief. The policeman walked back to the filing cabinet. He pulled a roll of paper towels out of the same drawer he took the lubricant from and tossed it to Juntaro.

"Clean up, and make it quick. I'm going to go get your friend," the policeman said.

As the policeman left the room, Juntaro wiped the cum off his ass and the floor. He picked up his torn panties. They were too shredded to put back on. He tossed the paper towels and the panties in the trash can and gathered up everything that had been dumped out of his purse.

He hung his purse back over his shoulder and as he was straightening his skirt, the policeman opened the door.

"All right. Come on, girly."

ONE TWO THREE FOUR!

Juntaro stood in the hallway of the police station with the heavyset policeman. He looked at the policeman, who stoically gazed forward without casting a glance back. Juntaro blushed. He thought that he should probably feel humiliated about what just happened, but he didn't. That was the best sexual encounter he'd had in a long time. It reminded him of the SM shows he did with Tetsuya when he started his career. He worried about Kotono, but recalled seeing how young and inexperienced the policeman that arrested her looked. He figured that her questioning couldn't have been very harsh.

After a moment, the younger policeman led Kotono from the room she was in toward them. Juntaro immediately noticed that Konoto's head was hanging and there was a limp in her step. The young policeman walked next to her like everything was normal.

"Kotono?" Juntaro said. "Are you okay?"

Kotono looked up at him. She had an odd, glazed expression on her face.

"All right, you two," the heavyset policeman said. "Get lost."

"I think something's wrong with her," Juntaro said.

"I said get lost. If you aren't out of here in thirty seconds, we're booking you for trespassing."

Juntaro grabbed Kotono's arm and hurried her out the front door of the station. As he led her down the stairs, Kotono tripped and would have fallen had Juntaro not been holding on to her arm.

"Kotono, what's wrong? What happened in there?" Juntaro said.

Kotono brought her head up again. The same glazed look was plastered on her face.

"What do you mean?" she said. She mumbled her words as if she'd just woken up.

"That cop, what did he do to you?"

"He just brought me into that room to ask about the bartender."

"What did he do to you? Did he beat you? Give you drugs?"

"I don't think so."

"What happened to you? Why do you look so sick?"

"I don't know. I think I missed it."

"Are you going to be okay?"

"I don't know."

A police car pulled up in front of the station. Two tall, muscular policemen who looked like they could have been twin brothers got out. They pulled an unconscious man in a blue flannel shirt and jeans out of the back seat. His face was bleeding from the nose and mouth. Both his eyes were blackened and his forehead was covered in bruises. Juntaro felt his stomach roil when he saw the man's face. The policemen picked him up under the arms and started carrying him into the station. They stopped when they saw Juntaro and Kotono.

"Hey," one of the policemen said. "Do you girls need something?"

"I think my friend is sick," Juntaro said, feeling extremely nervous that he had their attention.

"Well, this isn't a hospital," the other policeman said. He pointed up the street. "There's a doctor's office that way."

The two policemen carried their injured prisoner into the station. Juntaro looked around. Like the bar, the police station seemed to have been randomly set down in an industrial area. Rather than office or government buildings like a police station in Tokyo would have, it was surrounded by factories, silos, warehouses, and vacant lots. He tried to remember how to get back to where the police picked them up. Then Kotono's head slumped again. He realized that he needed to get her medical help before anything else. He put her arm around his shoulders and carried her in the direction the policeman had pointed.

ONE TWO THREE FOUR!

The two-story building looked like it had seen better days. The bricks were old and chipped in several places. One of the windows was broken out and covered in clear plastic. The neon sign advertising the nail salon on the bottom level flickered on and off like it was barely struggling to hang on. Juntaro couldn't even see the sign advertising a "Dr. O and Dr. D" on the second floor until he got close. Kotono's arm still around his shoulder, he carried her up the stairs and to the door, which also gave the doctors' names only as initials. To his surprise, it opened to a lit-up waiting room. He thought for sure the office would be closed at this late hour, but he had no idea where else to go.

The waiting room had the same sterile blandness as every other such room. White walls, chairs arranged in rows, tables with magazines on them, and a desk where the receptionist sat typing on her computer. Juntaro sat Kotono down in one of the chairs. Her head remained slumped and her arms hung limply at her side.

Juntaro went up to the receptionist's desk. The woman sitting behind it stood out from the otherwise normal-looking waiting room. She had pale white skin, heavy makeup, and shiny black hair. She wore a tight, low-cut nurse's uniform which showed off her ample cleavage. Her skirt was short and the stockings she wore were nearly as high as it, leaving a small gap that showed the flesh of her thigh. She looked more like an AV idol than any sort of nurse or receptionist.

"Excuse me," Juntaro said. "I'm sorry, but my friend is sick. She needs a doctor."

"You came to the right place," the receptionist said, smirking. "Dr. O is in. I'll go get him. Please have a seat."

The receptionist got up from her seat and headed into the back. Juntaro sat down next to Kotono, who looked to have fallen asleep. He checked her pulse and her breath. She seemed to be okay, just passed out. At least, he hoped so. The doctor would have to determine that when he examined her.

Juntaro picked up one of the magazines on the table in front of them without looking at the cover. He opened it and was greeted with a picture of a chubby woman with huge breasts and a pixelated cock in her mouth. The image didn't disgust him, but it did surprise him. He looked through the magazines on the table and realized that they were all Japanese porn.

The receptionist came back, buttoning up her top, apparently having taken it off for some reason.

"The doctor will be with you shortly," she said as she sat back at the computer and resumed typing.

Juntaro was beginning to doubt putting Kotono's well-being in the hands of whoever ran this office, but he still had no idea where else he could take her.

ONE TWO THREE FOUR!

Juntaro wasn't sure how long he and Kotono had been sitting in the waiting room. The only sound in the room was the receptionist typing or shuffling paper. At one point, Kotono woke up, weakly lifting her head.

"Where are we?" she said, mumbling so quietly he could barely understand.

"We're at a doctor's office. Don't worry. He's going to help you."

"Thank you, Jun. You're too kind. You're the nicest person . . ."

Kotono's head hung back down. Juntaro felt her pulse and breath again. She still seemed to be just asleep. Despite that, he was still worried about her. He wondered where that damn doctor was.

Juntaro grabbed an SM magazine off the table to try to distract himself. He looked through a photoset of a slim woman with her hair tied in pigtails. She was shown crawling on her hands and knees with a chubby man leading her around on a leash and a dog tail butt plug was in her anus. Juntaro had no sexual interest in women, but imagining himself in her place was very erotic to him.

His fantasizing was interrupted by the door to the back opening and the man who came through yelling, "Next patient!"

The man wore a black lab coat, black scrubs, and green rubber gloves. He had a head mirror on, which Juntaro hadn't seen on a doctor in years, and a stethoscope around his neck. Something about his face was off. It seemed like his skin and muscle wasn't wrapped correctly around his skull. His surgical mask obscured most of his face, but his eyes were the most off-putting thing. Juntaro couldn't put his finger on what it was about his eyes that bothered him though. Still, this had to be Dr. O and Kotono needed his help. Juntaro tapped Kotono on the shoulder.

"Kotono, the doctor's ready for you," he said.

She didn't even stir in her sleep. He shook her gently.

"Kotono? You need to get up."

She still didn't move.

"Next patient!" the doctor said more impatiently.

Juntaro put Kotono's arm around his shoulder and picked her up. She followed his steps, indicating that she was conscious on some level but apparently not able to get up on her own. He followed Dr. O into the back. The hall was much longer than Juntaro would have thought from the outside. Dr. O brought them to an examination room through one of the doors toward the end. The walls were just as white as the waiting room, but every piece of furniture, the cabinets, the chairs, the examination table, the trim on the window, were all bright blue, red, or yellow. It looked to Juntaro like someone had gotten their interior design inspiration from a Piet Mondrian painting.

Juntaro set Kotono up on the table and let her lie down. The doctor pointed at a chair against the wall without saying anything. Juntaro sat down.

The doctor leaned over her with his hands behind his back, looking closely at Kotono's face. He grabbed her under the chin and turned her head on each side, feeling the scars on her cheeks. He took a small flashlight, held her eyelids open, and examined each of her eyes. He turned around and faced Juntaro with his hands still behind his back.

"It's obvious to me that this girl has been attacked by a rabid red panda, resulting in massive tears in the buccinator and masseter muscles," Dr. O said. "The rabies has clearly infected the fine girl severely."

"That's not what happened at all!" Juntaro said. "She's had those scars on her face a long time. She didn't get sick until tonight."

Dr. O stared at Juntaro for a moment, looked back at Kotono, and then back at Juntaro.

"Oh yes," he said. "You're right. So tell me what happened to this girl."

Juntaro explained what happened at the police station.

"I see," Dr. O said.

His arms still behind his back, the doctor walked a lap around the examination table, keeping his gaze fixed on Kotono. He leaned back into her face and opened her mouth, taking his flashlight and shining it inside. He turned her face on her side again and looked in her ear with the flashlight. After staring in her ear for a moment, he stuck the earpieces of the stethoscope in his own and held the diaphragm to her forehead, nodding as he seemed to realize what the problem was. He placed the stethoscope back around his neck.

"I see," he said. "It's obvious the patient is suffering from a medullary double fracture."

"Um. What does that mean?"

"It means that she needs a bad operation."

The doctor walked over to the cabinet and pulled open one of the drawers. He plucked out a scalpel. He examined it as if he was making sure it was sharp enough. He seemed very excited at the prospect of getting to use it.

Juntaro jumped out of his seat and hurried over to Kotono. He started lifting her off the examination table. Now he didn't care if there was anywhere else to go. He'd take his chances rather than let this obvious quack dig that scalpel into her.

"We'll come back for that later," Juntaro said.

"But there's not much time," Dr. O said. "The carcinomic fungi are spreading in her vascular oblongata at an alarming rate."

Juntaro didn't answer back. He carried Kotono over his shoulder down the hall and back into the waiting room as fast as he could. As he made a beeline for the door, the secretary called out to him.

"Thank you for coming and have a nice day!" she said.

Juntaro ignored her. He carried his friend out the door and down the stairs. As he was descending, Kotono still seemed to have only the barest of awareness of what was happening. He suddenly realized why Dr. O's eyes bothered him so much. The entire time, he never blinked or moved them in their sockets once.

ONE TWO THREE FOUR!

Juntaro was relieved when he came to another bus stop bench. He sat Kotono down and took a seat next to her. He checked her pulse and breath. Both seemed fine despite the fact he couldn't get a response out of her. He wasn't sure what to do. He had no idea who in this town he could trust to take care of her. Would he have to carry her like this all the way back to Tokyo and get her to a hospital there?

Juntaro looked around. The bus stop was in front of a wide vacant lot strewn with garbage. Across the street, a factory exhaled smoke into the air from its stack. The smell of burning from it was strong. The bus stop sign gave no information just like that last one, but this one had been defaced with the word "kuso." He reached into Kotono's pocket and took out her phone. It read 2:30 a.m. He couldn't believe that little time had passed since they got on the train. He wished he had anyone's number memorized so he could call for help. He realized the only number he remembered off the top of his head was Tetsuya's, and there was nothing he could do where he was.

"Is your friend okay?" a croaking voice said to him.

Juntaro looked up. The homeless man they had passed earlier was standing there with his filthy bag slung over his shoulder.

The smell that he thought was coming from the factory was really coming from him.

"I don't know," Juntaro said. "I tried taking her to a doctor, but he didn't seem to know what he was doing."

"I saw the police pick you up," the homeless man said. "Is that why she's passed out?"

"Yes! I don't know what they did to her, but she's been out of it since they let us go."

"I've seen this happen to many of the people they've arrested. I might be able to help."

"Really?"

The homeless man nodded. He set his bag on the ground and rummaged through it, pulling out what appeared to be a sake bottle with the label peeled off. He shook the bottle and pulled the cap off.

"Could you tilt her head back?" the homeless man said. "I need to pour this in her mouth."

"What is that?" Juntaro said.

"It's a type of medicine."

"Are you sure?"

The homeless man handed the bottle to Juntaro.

"Feel free to try it yourself," the homeless man said. "It won't affect you."

Juntaro took the bottle and sniffed it. The fluid inside had very little odor, just a vague scent of alcohol. He poured a dab on his finger and licked it off. The taste was the same. It was like heavily watered-down vodka. While he still doubted it would help Kotono, he decided that it likely wouldn't harm her. It was worth a try.

"I can hold her head back while you give it to her," the homeless man said.

He did so, holding Kotono's mouth open with his fingers as well. Juntaro slowly poured the clear liquid into her mouth.

A moment after it hit her tongue, her head jerked forward. She started coughing and spitting.

"God!" she said. "What did you give me? That was the worst thing I've ever tasted!"

"Kotono?" Juntaro said. "Are you feeling okay?"

Kotono spit a few more times. She looked around.

"I think I am. Where are we? I remember the police picking us up and then nothing until you woke me up with that awful stuff."

Juntaro explained what happened after the police let them go, the strange doctor, and the homeless man's medicine. Kotono stood, turned to the homeless man, and bowed.

"Thank you so much!" she said, before turning to Juntaro and bowing again. "I'm so sorry about what happened! I don't know what that policeman did to me."

"The interrogation techniques used here are very harsh," the homeless man said, taking the bottle back from Juntaro. "Many of my friends have been through the same thing. As far as I can tell, this medicine is the only thing that brings people out of their catatonic state."

"What exactly do they do?" Kotono said. "I can't remember a thing."

"I don't know. No one who's been subjected to it remembers it. The medicine was given to me by a doctor who has since disappeared."

Juntaro stood up and bowed to the homeless man.

"Thank you very much," he said. "I'm sorry I didn't trust you at first."

The homeless man smiled, revealing his black teeth.

"I understand," he said. "There aren't many you can trust in this world. Even the ones we've been raised to believe we have to trust."

"I'm more convinced of that than ever."

"I hate to ask more from you," Kotono said, bowing. "But can you tell us what city this is? We got here by mistake and we can't find our way home."

"You're nowhere."

"What? We have to be somewhere"

"No. You're in Dokonimo. That's the name of the city."

"I've never heard of it before."

"How far away from Tokyo are we?" Juntaro said.

"That I'm afraid I can't tell you," the homeless man said. "I've never been outside of this city my entire life. I know very few who've left as well."

"We got here by train. There has to be one out."

"The only trains here haven't run for years. Not officially anyway. Though there are rumors of trains that go in and out of the city."

"They aren't just rumors," Kotono said. "We rode here on one that came from Tokyo."

"I see," the homeless man said. "Was that in a warehouse near the Goodnight Work 36 bar?"

"Yes! That's where we were when we arrived."

"I see. I'd heard the rumors, but I could never enter the door the train was said to be through. It was always locked and too strong to break down."

"We could try seeing if we can get back to that train," Juntaro said to Kotono. "It has to loop back around to Tokyo."

"I don't know about that," Kotono said. "Genzo or the conductor might still be there. I don't want to run into them."

"Genzo, you say?" the homeless man said. "Another train is rumored to be under an abandoned building that used to be called the Genzo Plaza Hotel."

"That naming can't be a coincidence," Kotono said.

"Perhaps not. You may have more luck with that one, though. I'm afraid I can't confirm it's there. I've never checked that building."

Juntaro reached into his purse and pulled out the paper that was given to him in the bar. He handed it to the homeless man.

"Someone at Goodnight Work 36 gave me this," he said. "Do you know where this would lead?"

The homeless man read the paper. He nodded.

"Looks like the person who gave you this had the same idea," he said. "This would lead to the same abandoned hotel I told you about."

"Can you tell us how to get there from here?" Juntaro said. "With the police picking us up, I don't know where we are now."

"Certainly. I can lead you there if you'd like."

"We wouldn't want to trouble you," Kotono said.

"It's no trouble at all," the homeless man said. "After all, I have nowhere else to be."

ONE TWO THREE FOUR!

Juntaro and Kotono followed behind the homeless man.

"Are you sure we should be following him?" Kotono said quietly to Juntaro. "I know he helped me out, but following a stranger got us here in the first place."

"I know," Juntaro said. "But what choice do we have? Wander the city until we get to this hotel by accident?"

Kotono nodded.

"That's true," she said. "That would be way worse."

"I think we can actually trust this man."

"We take a left up here," the homeless man said.

"I'm sorry," Juntaro said. "I didn't ask your name."

"Masakatsu," he said. "And you two?"

Juntaro and Kotono gave him their names, Juntaro calling himself Jun just as he did to Kotono.

"It's been a long time since I've introduced myself by name," Masakatsu said. "There are very few who care to know who a bum is."

"That is true," Juntaro said.

"You've done so much for us," Kotono said. "If you don't mind me asking, why are you living on the street? You seem very smart."

"Intelligence counts for little in most of this world," Masakatsu said. "And as for why I'm on the street, I've always been here. I was for as long as I remember. My mother was homeless and I never knew my father. I've known no other life."

"I'm sorry. That sounds awful."

"Perhaps it does to you. To a bird a life without flight would seem awful, but does it to you? You've only known a life on the ground. I've never felt a desire to live any other way."

"Don't you want to have a comfortable bed to sleep in? Money to spend on food? You see people with that every day and you don't want it?"

"There are times when I envy other people, but not often. I don't mean to say my life is better than theirs, or that my way is the most desirable. Many others I've known have taken to living on the street for incredibly tragic reasons and know nothing but misery. But to me, there is freedom in it. I see so many men and women going into those factories in the morning and out in the evening. There's no light in their eyes. They go to the bars to drink themselves numb. They don't even look each other in the eye as they walk the street. To me, a life chasing those comforts is far worse than the life of freedom that I have now."

Kotono nodded.

"I see what you mean," she said. "As much as I'm not always happy with my life, I don't think I'd want one without a job or a home."

"I wouldn't recommend it to many," Masakatsu said. "It's an often very dangerous life. In the past week, two men who I shared a camp with have turned up dead. It was clear they were murdered."

"Oh my god! I'm so sorry!"

"Very brutal murders too. They turned up with many stab wounds and limbs missing. The newspaper says that a serial killer is responsible. I'm being very cautious."

"If it is a serial killer, maybe they killed the bartender too," Juntaro said to Kotono.

"I don't know about that," she said. "I've read a lot about serial killers. They tend to stick to a pattern. If he was killing homeless people, then the bartender doesn't fit his MO."

"I assume you mean the owner of Goodnight Work 36?" Masakatsu said.

"That's him," Juntaro said. "The police arrested us because we were the last ones there before he was killed."

"I see. You're lucky to have gotten away. The police here prefer to place blame on the first person they suspect. Many of my friends have been in and out of jail because of that."

Juntaro jumped as he heard the blaring horn and a shout from a car coming from behind them on the street. He whipped his head around and saw a beat-up old Toyota coming toward them. Keith was hanging his head out the window and waving at him. He stopped the car next to them.

"Well, hello there, pretty girls!" Keith said.

Juntaro smiled at him. Kotono regarded him with the same stony distrust as before.

"Hello, Keith!" Juntaro said. "It's good to see you again!"

"Do you and your new hobo friend need a ride?"

"It's okay," Kotono said. "Masakatsu here is getting us home."

"Well, all of you can hop on in! I'll get you there faster."

Juntaro leaned over to Kotono.

"I think we'll be okay riding with him," he said quietly to her. "I don't think there's anything wrong with him. If there is, it's three against one. I want to get home just as badly as you do."

"Okay," Kotono said. "But we should all sit in the back."

Juntaro nodded. Kotono turned to Masakatsu.

"Are you okay with riding with him?" she said.

"If this young man doesn't mind a hobo in his car," Masakatsu said.

"It's no problem at all!" Keith said. "Come on in!"

Juntaro opened the door to the back seat. He climbed in and Kotono followed him. She motioned Masakatsu to come in the back with them. He sat down as well, putting his bag on his lap.

"One of you can come in the front if you're crowded back there," Keith said, looking at his passengers in the rearview mirror.

"We're okay," Kotono said.

Keith winced, Masakatsu's body odor apparently having just hit him.

"Damn," Keith said. "You need a wash, son. Keep your window rolled down."

ONE TWO THREE FOUR!

Keith drove the beat-up Toyota, following the directions that Masakatsu gave him from the back seat to the Genzo Plaza Hotel. Occasionally, he took a drink from a bottle of something labeled "Yoo-hoo." Juntaro had never seen the drink before, but it looked to him like chocolate milk.

Juntaro watched the city through the window. It made him wonder if the city planners were all alcoholics. The more he saw of it, the more haphazard it seemed put together. A relatively new-looking 7-Eleven was sitting between a vacant lot and a factory that looked like it had been out of operation for years. What looked like a discrete love hotel sat next to a plant belching thick smoke into the air. Juntaro couldn't imagine trying to have sex in a place like that. A warehouse whose parking lot contained several gaudy, brightly lit dekotora was next to a construction site with a sign advertising apartments coming soon. He began to feel more empathy than before for the people he'd seen here, even the bartender and the crazy doctor. He also felt a great admiration for Masakatsu. Dokonimo must be hell to live in, especially on the streets.

"So," Keith said. "What have you girls been up to tonight?"

"Nothing," Kotono said.

"Sounds like a fun time!"

Juntaro giggled. He told Keith about the bartender and the police picking them up.

"Really? The barkeep's dead?" Keith said. "He was a dick, though. I'm not surprised someone wanted him dead."

"He did have a wife, you know," Kotono said.

"Well, I do feel for her. What happened after the cops got you two ladies?"

Juntaro lied and told him that he convinced the police to let them go after telling them what really happened. He told them about the state Kotono was in and the doctor's office he took her to.

"Whoah, whoah, wait," Keith said. "You said his name was Dr. O?"

"Is that your friend you were looking for?"

"Yes! That's him! You've got to show me where that office is!"

"Now?" Kotono said.

"I'll take you to that hotel, I promise. But I've got to go see Dr. O. I've been searching for him for so damn long," Keith said, the excitement obvious in his voice.

"Okay," Juntaro said. "We just need to get to the police station and I can direct you from there. Masakatsu, do you know how to get there from here?"

Keith turned the car around, following the new directions that his guide in the back seat was giving him.

ONE TWO THREE FOUR!

Keith passed the police station and continued down the street until Juntaro pointed out the building where Dr. O's office was. He stopped the car in front of the building and got out, leaving the key in the ignition.

"I'm just going to go up, get reacquainted, and get his contact info," Keith said. "You all make yourself at home, listen to the radio, just don't do anything I wouldn't. I'll be right back down."

He sprinted toward the building, running up the steps so fast that Juntaro could hear his feet pounding like a drum beat.

"Do you mind if I turn on the radio?" Kotono said.

"Yes, I could use some music," Juntaro said.

"What do you want to listen to?"

"You go ahead and pick."

"Is there anything specific you like?" Kotono said to Masakatsu.

"Oh, no," he said. "I rarely have a chance to listen to music. I have no preference."

Kotono reached in the front and turned the power knob on the radio. Static came on. She hit the tuning button. The station that came on played a pop song that was sung in what sounded to Juntaro like Khmer. He wondered how a Cambodian station was being picked up, especially this clearly. Kotono hit the tuning button again and Juntaro found himself even more confused. A

station identification for NHK Radio 1 was coming in, but was
distorted by static. Where in Japan was this city that the radios
could pick up stations in Cambodia loud and clear but not its own
country's public broadcasting?

Kotono hit the tuning button again and this time a song being
played on piano came through. Juntaro recognized it as a jazz
composition being played by Ryo Fukui. There was still a slight
distortion from the radio static but he found that it made the
song even more enjoyable. Kotono must have agreed because she
leaned back and took in the sound of the music. She reached in her
pocket, took out her phone, and flipped it open. Juntaro looked at
the time. It read 3:17 a.m. He wondered if he and Kotono would
be back in Tokyo before dawn.

ONE TWO THREE FOUR!

"How long has your foreign friend been in there?" Masakatsu said.

Kotono took her phone out of her pocket and opened it. Juntaro saw that it read 3:48 a.m. The entire time the three of them had been sitting in the back seat quietly listening to the jazz music on the radio, which was now playing a Masayoshi Takanaka song, the station never stopped the music for identification or commercials, which Juntaro was only now noticing. The closest thing to anything eventful happening as they were waiting was Masakatsu getting out to go around to the back of the building to urinate.

"It's been almost an hour," she said. "Maybe one of us should go up and see what's keeping him."

Juntaro thought for a moment.

"I think we should all go," Juntaro said. "You were passed out while we were there, but that doctor was really off. I don't want any one of us to be in there alone."

"You think he's dangerous?" Kotono said.

"I don't think so, but I don't want to take that chance."

"Do you know anything about that doctor's office?" Kotono said to Masakatsu.

"I'm afraid I don't," he said. "I only recently saw it open."

"He is a friend of Keith's, so I'm sure he's okay," Juntaro said to Kotono. "But after the way he acted while examining you, I have a very bad feeling about him."

"Okay," Kotono said. "Let's go."

Juntaro reached in the front, pulled the key out of the ignition, and put it in his purse.

ONE TWO THREE FOUR!

Juntaro was the first to enter the office with Masakatsu behind him and Kotono coming in last. The receptionist wasn't at her desk. The waiting room was the same as before, except the door to the back was hanging open.

"Keith? Are you here?" Juntaro called out.

There was no response.

"He must be through there," Masakatsu said, pointing at the door to the back.

Juntaro had a bad feeling. He thought maybe it was because of everything that had happened, but he wondered if going back there was a bad idea. He looked through the door and saw nothing unusual, except that the door to the examining room that he previously brought Kotono to was open. He led her and Masakatsu down the hall.

He looked into the examination room. There didn't seem to be anyone in the room. He was about to turn away when he looked to the corner. The receptionist was on the floor in a puddle of blood. Her eyes were rolled back in her head and her face was frozen in a death mask of fear and pain. There was a deep red gash in her throat. Her dress was torn open and a gaping hole filled with torn fatty tissue on her chest showed that one of her breasts had been violently hacked off.

Juntaro started at the sight and backed up into the wall behind him.

"What's wrong, Jun?" Masakatsu said.

Juntaro couldn't get the words out. He just pointed into the room at the receptionist's mutilated body. Kotono and Masakatsu looked into the room. Masakatsu slapped his hand over his mouth in fear and disgust. Kotono let out a terrified shriek.

Juntaro was about to turn and run back down the hallway, but one of the doors opened and Keith emerged. He was covered head to toe in blood. In one hand he held a bloody butcher knife. In the other he held the receptionist's severed breast, his fingers dug in the fatty tissue like a bowling ball. The charming smile was gone from his face, replaced with a demented rictus.

"Sorry girls," Keith said. "I didn't want you to have to see this."

"What the hell is going on!" Juntaro said. It was far more of a panicked outburst than an actual question.

"I only came up here to kill Dr. O. The girl just got in the way."

Keith held up the severed breast.

"I was hoping to take this for dinner tomorrow," he said. "Breast meat is delicious."

Juntaro turned and was about to run. He didn't know what was through the door at the end of the hall, but he hoped it was a way out. Then the door opened and Dr. O stepped out. Juntaro was almost relieved to see him, but then he noticed the doctor's eyes were gone. The creepy, unmoving eyes above his surgical mask had been replaced by two black voids. It almost kept him from noticing that he was also holding a brightly colored gun that looked like a kid's toy. When Kotono saw his face, she let out another scream.

"Your face is nothing to look at either, young lady," Dr. O said.

"There you are, motherfucker!" Keith said. "I'm killing your ass for good this time!"

"You're starting to annoy me."

"You ran all the way to fucking Japan to get away from me, you scary-ass bitch!"

"You interfere far too much with my work."

"Work this, asshole!"

Keith threw the butcher knife. It flew past Juntaro, barely missing him, and lodged into Dr. O's chest. The doctor grunted as the knife went into him. A purple fluid started leaking from the wound. He looked at the knife in him, touching the gash and looking at the fluid on his hand as if to confirm he really was injured.

Without saying a word, Dr. O raised the colorful weapon in his hand and pulled the trigger. A loud, high-pitched squeal came from the gun and a beam of light shot out from the barrel. It flew past Kotono, missing her head and shoulder and hitting the wall next to Keith. It left a black hole as if fire had been shot through it. Before anyone had a chance to react, the doctor fired again. This time the beam hit Masakatsu in his side, leaving a gaping, charred black wound. He screamed, clutching his side, and fell to the ground. The hall instantly smelled of burnt flesh.

"No!" Juntaro yelled.

He and Kotono dove to the floor, crawling to Maskatasu to cover him. He was writhing and moaning in pain. The doctor fired again, this time the beam barely missed Keith's head. Keith fell to his knees, dropping the severed breast in his hand. He reached under his belt and pulled out a hunting knife.

Dr. O aimed and fired again. This time the high-pitched squeal came out but no beam. He looked down the barrel with his empty eye socket, pointed it down, and beat the side of the gun. He aimed it again, but Keith was already on him, having jumped over the three taking cover on the hallway floor. He slashed at the doctor's hand. The gun fell to the floor. A blue fluid leaked from the doctor's slashed hand onto his green rubber gloves. Dr. O swung his other hand. His fist connected with Keith's cheek. As Keith stumbled back, he slashed again. He made a gash in Dr. O's stomach. This time a green liquid stained the doctor's black scrubs. Through his fear and confusion, Juntaro wondered how many colors of blood the doctor had in him. Kotono held Masakatsu, trying to comfort him through his pain.

Dr. O reached into his scrub pocket and pulled out a scalpel. He pointed the blade out toward Keith.

"*En garde!*" Dr. O said.

"*Fuck you!*" Keith said in English.

Dr. O lunged at Keith with the blade. Keith dodged to the side and slashed up, slicing the doctor's face up the middle. Rather than bleed any kind of fluids, his face started peeling apart. He grabbed the back of his head and, with one pull, everything on his head slid off, revealing a bare skull. Juntaro was terrified, but not surprised at the sight. He looked over at Kotono. Her head was down as she held Masakatsu, whispering in his ear that he was going to be okay.

"*Shit!*" Dr. O said in English.

He swung his arm around Keith and stabbed the scalpel into his back. Keith howled as the blade planted in his spine. Dr. O twisted the scalpel, making Keith cry out in pain even more. Keith rammed his forehead into Dr. O's face, knocking a couple teeth out of the skull that was now the doctor's face. Dr. O went down with Keith on top of him.

"*I always knew you were a backstabbing bitch!*" Keith said in English.

He brought his hunting knife down into the doctor's torso repeatedly. Yellow, black, red, green, and purple liquids flowed from the wounds. He pulled the other knife out of Dr. O's chest and brought both down on the doctor with each hand, one after the other. He kept stabbing until the doctor stopped moving and grunting with each stab.

As Keith was on top of the doctor, Juntaro quietly got up and opened the door closest to him. It led to another examination room. He tapped Kotono on the shoulder and pointed into the room. Kotono looked up with tears in her eyes and nodded. They both grabbed Masakatsu at opposite ends and carried him carefully into the room. They set him down gently on the examination table.

Juntaro looked out in the hall. He saw that Keith was sawing the doctor's skull head off his apparently lifeless body. He shut the door and barricaded it with one of the chairs.

ONE TWO THREE FOUR!

"Masakatsu!" Kotono said. "Can you hear me?"

Masakatsu nodded and wheezed.

Juntaro grabbed Masakatsu's jacket and tried to lift it up to look at the wound. It caught where the wound was and Masakatsu squirmed and cried out in pain. Whatever came out of that gun had fused his coat to his skin.

"I'm sorry!" Juntaro said. "I know a little first aid, but it's been a long time since I learned it. I don't know what to do with this."

"I need to call 119," Kotono said, taking her phone out of her pocket.

"No, don't," Maskatsu said. "I know I'm not going to make it. The police will get involved and blame you for my death."

"Don't talk like that! You'll make it!"

"No, no. I really know I'm not going to."

Masakatsu coughed.

"I can see things," he said. "It comes at random. Sometimes it's what's in people's heads, sometimes it's the future. The things I told you I had heard as rumors were things I had seen that way."

He smirked.

"Such a useless gift, isn't it?" he said. "I didn't see I was going to die until right after that thing hit me."

"That can't be," Juntaro said. "Kotono, call the ambulance."

"Please," Masakatsu said. "Don't call anyone, Juntaro."

"Juntaro?" Kotono said.

Juntaro stood for a moment staring at the injured man on the table. He motioned for Kotono to put her phone down.

"He's telling the truth," Juntaro said.

"We can't just let you die!" Kotono said.

"It's okay," Masakatsu said. "I knew I was destined for an early death. It comes with the life I've lived. Dying this way with two beautiful women is far better than dying alone on the street."

"How are the police going to blame us?" Juntaro said. "The lunatics responsible are right outside this door. In the condition they're in, there's no way they can escape."

As if on cue, a loud muffled shattering came from the hallway. Juntaro put his ear to the door. It sounded like the hallway had gone dead silent.

"Wait right here," Juntaro said. "I'm going to check the hall. Put the chair back up behind me. I'll knock once when I come back."

"Are you sure that's a good idea?" Kotono said.

"Don't worry, it sounds like they aren't a threat anymore," he said. "I just want to make sure we're safe."

Kotono nodded. Juntaro took the chair away from the door and walked into the hall. He closed the door behind him.

Juntaro looked left and right. Dr. O lay dead on the floor, his skull head severed in a multicolored pool that resembled oily water. The hunting knife was stuck in his chest and the butcher knife through one of his eye sockets. Keith was gone, but a trail of red blood led to the door at the end of the hall, which was hanging open.

Juntaro walked down to the hall, stepping around the doctor's mutilated body, and peeked his head inside the room. It appeared to be an office. The entire floor seemed to be covered in pelts from lions, tigers, zebras, pumas, and bears instead of carpeting. Where another doctor may have had paintings, charts, or degrees, the wall was covered in posters of nude women of various races. Most of them had the women bent over or on all fours showing off their big asses. The bookshelves, instead of being full of medical texts, were full of porn films in DVD, VHS, and even Betamax formats. Some were professionally made, while others were clear bootlegs with their obscene names written on the spines in marker. The ornate desk was the only thing that looked like it belonged. On it was a closed laptop and two globes, one of Earth and the other of what looked to Juntaro like Jupiter. The window behind the desk was completely shattered, the cool night air blowing in from outside.

Juntaro saw on the floor where the trail of blood led around the desk. He followed it and looked down. There was a splash of blood where it looked like someone had made impact with the pavement. He looked around and saw what looked like Keith crawling around the corner to the front of the building.

Juntaro ran back down the hall into the waiting room, jumping over Dr. O's body like a hurdle. He grabbed one of the chairs and blocked the door. He knew there was no way Keith had the strength to climb the stairs, but he wasn't taking any chances. He ran back to the room where Kotono and Masakatsu were and knocked on the door.

He took another look at Dr. O's body. He saw that the scrubs covered in multicolor blood were still sprawled on the floor, as were the headlamp and gloves, but the body itself was gone. Juntaro looked around, hoping that whatever kind of creature the doctor was had just dissolved when it died and that it wasn't still alive.

Juntaro went back to the door to the room with his two friends and knocked. Kotono opened the door and let Juntaro back in, closing the door and putting the chair back against it behind him.

Masakatsu was still on the examining table with his eyes closed.

"How is he?" Juntaro said.

"He's still alive, but he seems to be getting worse," Kotono said.

Juntaro checked his signs. His breathing was shallow and his pulse was weak. Juntaro sighed.

"Are those two out there dead?" Kotono said.

"The doctor's dead," Juntaro said. "Keith threw himself out a window, that's what the shattering was. I don't know why. I think he was trying to escape. If he's not dead yet, he will be soon. I'm sorry, Kotono. You were right. We shouldn't have trusted him."

"At least he killed the thing that did this," she said, pointing to Masakatsu.

Juntaro looked at the wound.

"I'm going to try something," Juntaro said. "I don't know if it will help, but I feel bad about just leaving him."

Juntaro looked through the cabinets in the room until he found gauze and antiseptic. He poured the antiseptic on the gauze and placed it gently against Masakatsu's wound. Masakatsu jolted awake, taking a deep breath through clenched teeth.

"I'm sorry!" Juntaro said. "Does that hurt?"

Masakatsu nodded.

"It's okay," he said. "I appreciate the thought, but it's not going to help. If you can find something for the pain, that would be much better."

Juntaro went through the cabinets again. He found a drawer full of pill bottles. He checked each one until he found one labeled as codeine. Per the recommendations on the instructions, he took two pills from the bottle. He got a paper cup from the dispenser next to the sink, filled it up, and brought it all to Masakatsu. Masakatsu tossed the pills in his mouth and drank the entire cup.

"I've always avoided medications like this," he said. "I've seen too many people on the street addicted to them, too many arrested and never coming back when the police caught them."

"I hope it helps," Juntaro said.

"If you wouldn't mind, could you two hold my hands? I'm going to go back to sleep. I don't think I'm going to wake up."

Juntaro and Kotono did as he asked. Masakatsu closed his eyes. Shortly after, Juntaro felt his grip weaken and then go slack.

ONE TWO THREE FOUR!

Kotono started crying quietly when she saw Maskatsu slipping away. Juntaro reached down and put the deceased's hands to his side to give him a dignified look.

"I think we should say a prayer," Juntaro said.

Kotono nodded, tears running down her cheeks. The two of them bowed and clapped their hands, praying for their friend. After they finished, they looked down at his body for a moment.

"Should we try to bury him somewhere?" Kotono said.

"I don't think so," Juntaro said. "I'd like to give him a proper funeral, but we can't risk carrying around a dead body here."

"You're right."

"We'd better get out of here in case anyone heard the noise and called the police."

Juntaro moved the chair from the door and walked into the hall. Kotono followed him. She looked at the pile of clothes and equipment where Dr. O's body was.

"Where did he go?" Kotono said.

"It's okay," Juntaro said. "His body dissolved when he died. I saw it."

"What was he? A monster?"

"I have no idea. I'm just glad he's dead."

Juntaro felt a little bad about lying to her, but after Masakatsu's death, he wanted to reassure her. The two of them walked into the waiting room. Juntaro closed the door behind them.

"What do we do now?" Kotono said.

"I still have the key to Keith's car," Juntaro said. "I say we drive until we can find the hotel. It can't be that far away."

"Well, we don't have anywhere else to go."

Juntaro moved the chair from the waiting room door and he and Kotono headed down the stairs. He was hoping he'd see Keith's body in front of the building. He really wanted some confirmation the man was dead and wouldn't bother them again.

When they got down to the car, Keith's body was nowhere to be found but the driver seat door was open. Based on the trail of blood on the ground, Juntaro could tell that Keith had crawled to the car and then away when he saw the key was gone.

He reassured Kotono that there was no way that Keith would survive that blade in his spine and the fall, but he wasn't sure himself.

ONE TWO THREE FOUR!

Juntaro started the car. The radio came on playing a Sun Ra song. Kotono sat in the front seat with her feet resting on the pile of garbage on the floor. There was a lot in the small space. Boxes from doughnut shops, Yoo-hoo bottles like the half-finished one sitting in the cupholder, colorful pill bottles that had a Western cartoon character that Juntaro recognized as Fred Flintstone, a crushed box for adult diapers, and a torn-up Apple Jacks cereal box. He didn't blame Kotono for looking disgusted as she sat down.

"You can sit in the back," Juntaro said.

"No, no," she said. "I'll be fine. Why did we trust him in the first place? Everything about him was weird."

"He had a trustworthy face," Juntaro said. "I'm sorry. I should have been more cautious."

Kotono sighed.

"It's not that I hate foreign men," she said "I've just had too many bad experiences. This has to be the worst."

"He was a psychopath," Juntaro said as he put the car in gear and pulled it on the road. "Those exist everywhere."

"I guess you're right. Can I ask you something?"

Juntaro thought he probably already knew what she wanted to ask.

"Go ahead," he said.

"Why did Masakatsu call you Juntaro?"

"That's my real name."

"That's a male name. Is that why you call yourself Jun?"

"No, I'm actually a man."

"What?"

"I'm so sorry. I wasn't trying to fool you. I just didn't want you to think I was a crazy pervert."

"It's okay. I know you're not crazy. So I guess you're gay too?"

"I am, yes."

"Well, that's okay. It's a little weird, but who am I to say anything about that?"

She reached up and felt the scars on her cheeks.

"Besides," she said. "It's not like you're a serial killer or monster."

Juntaro and Kotono laughed together.

"I'm sorry," she said. "I shouldn't be laughing after what just happened."

"Well, humor is one way of dealing with situations like this. When my bandmate was in the hospital, he always told me jokes when I called or visited him. Even when his condition got worse. Even the last time I talked to him, the day before he died, he was laughing and joking like everything was going to be okay."

Kotono sighed.

"I'll feel better when I finally get home," she said.

Juntaro looked around as they passed the police station.

"Okay, I still have the instructions in my purse the guy in the bar gave me," he said. "If we can find our way back to the bar, we can head straight for that hotel."

ONE TWO THREE FOUR!

The streets of Dokonimo seemed even worse driving on than walking, especially when one didn't know where they were going. It was more apparent that several of the roads seemed to go on forever before they came to any sort of intersection. Several randomly ended in dead ends, forcing Juntaro to turn around constantly. Some were one-ways that he couldn't see marked as such until he'd been driving down them the wrong way for a couple miles. Too many things looked the same, giving him few markers to navigate by. Remembering the route the police took to the station from where they were picked up was a lot harder than he thought. On top of that, he didn't know how much gas was in the car. He watched the gauge, but it seemed to bounce up and down at random. It was clearly broken.

Juntaro was about to stop the car somewhere, anywhere, and beg for directions from someone when he saw the Goodnight Work 36 bar up the road. He handed his purse to Kotono.

"The directions are in there," he said.

Kotono dug through the purse, trying to find the paper.

"Are you sure?" she said.

"Oh, damn. Don't tell me I lost it."

"Wait, I think this is it."

She pulled out a crumpled piece of paper and smoothed it out.

"Yes!" she said. "Here it is!"

Juntaro breathed a sigh of relief. Maybe they would get home tonight after all.

ONE TWO THREE FOUR!

"It says to continue down this road," Kotono said. "The hotel is at the end of it."

"That was easier than I thought it would be," Juntaro said.

After everything, he expected the route to be full of bumps, both literal and figurative. At this point, he wouldn't have been surprised if the directions had turned out to be complete bullshit, though he really hoped that wasn't the case. The street it was taking them down seemed to have nothing. The buildings on either side were all either obviously abandoned or half demolished when there wasn't just a vacant lot. His fears were allayed when the street brought them to a large building that resembled two towers on top of a stone base. The sign over the entrance was missing parts, but he could tell it said "Genzo Plaza Hotel" at one time.

He parked the car as close as he could. He got out, taking the key just in case. Kotono got out on her side, accidentally kicking some of the trash out.

"Does your phone have plenty of battery?" he said. "We'll need it for light."

Kotono took out her phone and opened it. Juntaro looked at the screen. The time read 5:26 a.m. He realized that it should be dawn soon, but it was just as dark out as it was when they arrived.

"Looks like there's plenty of battery," Kotono said. "We're trying to find the basement, right? That shouldn't take too long."

"Let's hope so."

The two headed toward the hotel. The front door of the hotel surprisingly wasn't locked. It creaked loudly as Juntaro opened it. The musty smell hit him as soon as he stepped inside. It wasn't as dark inside as he expected, but something was off about the way it looked. Taking in everything around him was like looking at an old photograph even though it was all right in front of him. When he tried to comprehend what he saw, it was like something was blocking his mind from retaining it. He saw white walls, brown trim, a dirty floor, but he couldn't make out any details. He looked back and could see Kotono was confused by how everything looked as well. Like him, she was looking back outside to try to determine what seemed wrong. It had to be the hotel itself. Everything outside he could see looked normal.

"I don't know what it is," she said, "but I don't like it here."

"I don't either," he said. "But we spent all this time trying to get here. There's no point in turning back now."

"I know. Just stay close to me, okay?"

"Don't worry. I will."

Juntaro and Kotono walked farther into the abandoned hotel. It was like walking through a vague memory. Halls would pass by them like they were walking on a treadmill and the walls were part of a set for a play being moved by unseen stagehands. He would open doors without seeing his hand reach for them sometimes. Other times his hand, the feel of the knob, and the sound of the door opening would be the only things he perceived like the door he opened was invisible. Kotono stayed by his side but at times it looked like she was walking at impossible angles. He could swear that he saw her walk ahead of him a few times and dissolve into nothing, but then she'd still be next to him. He could see the fear on her face at times, but at others it looked like she had no expression whatsoever, like her face had suddenly become painted on.

The only thing that seemed consistent in the hotel was the smell. The must that reminded Juntaro of the flavor of blue cheese lingering in his mouth. The dust in the air was thick enough in a few rooms that he or Kotono would sneeze. Each time, it seemed like he heard the echo of the sneeze in some distant part of the hotel before he heard it from his or Kotono's mouth.

The entire time they walked, he wasn't sure where they were going. There were times where echoes of him telling Kotono or Kotono telling him they should try this way or that way came from a hallway or room they just passed through, though he would have sworn he never said them or heard them the first time around.

There were a few moments where he felt like he had walked away from himself and was now watching Kotono and himself walk from a distance. He would direct them as if they were video game characters and he were the player, though there was no controller in his hand. At random times, he would look around and think he saw Kotono and himself walking in an opposite direction or up on another floor.

Even though they were supposed to be going to the basement, they often felt compelled to go up a staircase. This would bring them to lower levels in the hotel. Somehow, he was aware where certain stairs, doors, or halls would take them. But not infallibly. They'd sometimes end up at a dead end, walk into a guest room or a bathroom, or go up staircases that never ended, forcing them to turn around and try another way.

Some degree of lucidity returned when he and Kotono ran into Genzo. He first appeared looking over the railing on one of the upper floors. He looked like the same nondescript Eidan worker at first, but then seemed to suddenly become twice his size. Juntaro looked again and realized that his whole body hadn't gotten larger, just his head, then his chest, then the feet running down the stairs after them. He then realized that whatever part of Genzo he was looking at seemed to project and become massive.

Genzo didn't say a word to him or Kotono, but Juntaro was immediately frightened of him and he could tell Kotono was too. For a while, Genzo simply chased after them. Then when they turned down a hallway, Genzo came running toward them, even though he was behind them just a moment ago. They turned and ran in the opposite direction.

Juntaro then realized that Genzo had grabbed Kotono by the hair. Her screaming echoed in the hallway. However, Juntaro was running toward them from behind as if the hallway looped around. He came at Genzo from behind and slammed his fist in the back of his head. He grabbed Kotono by the arm and led her out of the hallway.

Juntaro threw open a door and ran inside with Kotono in tow. As they ran toward another hallway, they realized that it was Genzo's mouth. Before they had a chance to turn around, it swallowed them. They ran in a dark void. Juntaro couldn't see anything, not even Kotono next to him. Then she took her phone out and flipped it open. The light from the screen illuminated her face. As the light from the screen cut through the dark, a screaming from Genzo surrounded them.

"It's hurting him!" Kotono said.

He heard it from her, but her mouth didn't move.

She waved the phone around, the light seeming to cut the darkness like a knife through a black sheet. Each time, Genzo screamed louder and louder. Finally, Kotono stabbed repeatedly down and a white doorway opened in the distance. Juntaro and Kotono ran toward it.

They emerged in a surprisingly well-lit hallway. In front of them, Genzo seemed to be flung down a stairway as they came through.

He continued screaming, until Juntaro heard a loud snap as he was halfway down the stairs. He reached the bottom and lay there.

Juntaro and Kotono slowly descended the stairs, keeping an eye on Genzo. When they reached his body, Juntaro knelt down to look at him. His neck was bent in an unnatural way. He'd obviously snapped it while he was falling down the stairs. Juntaro looked up at Kotono, who was visibly confused but said nothing.

Juntaro stood back up and looked around. He saw a door on the other side of the bare stone room they were in. The door was completely mismatched, looking more like the entrance to a subway car than one that would normally be found in a basement, but where the window would be was just solid black. He walked over to it and opened it. It led into the conductor's car of a subway train. He could see there was a tunnel lit by blue lights and a track through the front window of it.

"I think I found our train," Juntaro said.

"That can't be it," Kotono said. "Where's the rest of it?"

"I don't know. Let's just hope this gets us home."

ONE TWO THREE FOUR!

Juntaro sat in the driver seat. Kotono sat in the seat next to him. He looked over the control panel. It was a collection of buttons, knobs, and switches. There was also an intercom, though he didn't understand why it was there. There didn't seem to be any passenger cars to make announcements to.

"Do you know how to drive this thing?" Kotono said.

"I don't. Do you?" Juntaro said.

"I don't either."

"I guess we'll just have to improvise."

Juntaro pressed what looked to him like the button to start the train. He was right. There was a pounding noise and what sounded like power running through the car. He pushed a switch and the car started moving ahead slowly on the track.

"Whatever you're doing, it's working," Kotono said.

Juntaro pushed the switch and the car sped up. Kotono looked behind her at the door they came through. She got up and tried to open it. It was locked.

"And it looks like there's no going back," she said.

She sat back down and took her phone out of her pocket.

"This can't be right," she said.

"What's wrong?"

"It says that it's 5:30 a.m. There's no way that we were in that hotel for only four minutes."

"Maybe we were. Nothing seemed real in there. Maybe we were only in there for that long."

Kotono put her phone back in her pocket.

"Well," she said, "as long as this gets us back to Tokyo, I'm not going to let it bother me."

Juntaro pushed the switch to make it go a little faster. The subway train rumbled up the tracks.

"I don't know how fast I'm supposed to push it," he said. "If it's too fast, I won't be able to make the stop."

"Are those tunnel lights getting brighter?"

He'd been looking at the controls and trying to figure them out so he didn't see it at first, but she was right. The blue lights illuminating the tunnel got brighter and brighter as they moved along. Soon, the entire inside of the car seemed to be blue. They kept getting brighter. It was getting hard to see. Finally, the blue was bright enough that Juntaro had to shut his eyes to keep them from hurting.

"I can't see anything!" Kotono said. "What do we do? How will we know where to stop?"

"Maybe they'll dim as we go down the track," Juntaro said.

"It's starting to hurt even with my eyes closed!"

Juntaro put his hands over his eyes, even though he knew he should be keeping them on the controls. It helped at first, but the blue just kept getting brighter. The blue began hurting his head. It was like the blue was pushing past his eyes and drowning his brain. Kotono must have felt the same because she started screaming in pain.

"Kotono!" he cried out.

Finally, it was too much. He felt his consciousness slipping away. Everything was a painful deep blue and Kotono's screaming suddenly cut off. The last thing he heard before he passed out was what sounded like a crashing sound in the distance.

ONE TWO THREE FOUR!

"Juntaro!" Kotono's voice said. "Juntaro, wake up!"

Juntaro lifted his head up and opened his eyes. He felt like he was waking up from a deep, dreamless sleep. He realized he was sitting on a bench just outside the Shinjuku station. The sun was out and crowds of people were going in and out of the station. It didn't seem quite the same, though. It looked like some things had changed around since they left the night before. The Eidan logo had been replaced with a new one that read "Tokyo Metro." He noticed a lot more people had cell phones and were staring at them as they walked.

He looked at Kotono who was sitting next to him. It took him a moment to realize what was off about her. She looked like she had aged since he passed out in that subway.

"Kotono?" he said. "Are you okay?"

"I think I am," she said. "Are you?"

"I think so. How did we get here?"

"I don't know. I just remember all that blue and then passing out. Then we were both sitting here when I woke up."

"Everything looks kind of different. Are we really back in Tokyo?"

"I think we are, but look at this."

Kotono held her phone out for him. The time read 7:03 a.m. He was a little surprised that they were only out for an hour and a half. Then Kotono pointed out the date. The year read 2012. It was 2002 the previous night.

"That must be wrong," Kotono said. "The phone must be glitching or something. There's no way we were passed out for ten years."

Juntaro closed his eyes and shook his head. He reached into his purse, still flung around his shoulder, and pulled out a pocket mirror. He looked at his face. Like Kotono, he could tell that he had aged. There were bags under his eyes, his skin seemed paler and sicklier, and his hair seemed to have lost most of its sheen.

Juntaro slumped on the bench. He stared up at the sky. It was a friendly blue, unlike the painful blue that was in that subway tunnel, and clouds slowly drifted by.

"I don't know how," Juntaro said to Kotono. "But we were gone for ten years. That subway brought us back, along with the years we missed."

ONE TWO THREE FOUR!

Getting resituated after having disappeared for ten years was a little easier for Juntaro than he anticipated. A couple of his friends and collaborators had taken over the rent on his apartment when he hadn't been seen for a couple months. They kept it at first expecting he'd be back soon, then they started using it as a mini-studio, a rehearsal space, and a spot to crash. However, they always kept it clean and in order, hoping that Juntaro would be back some day, despite the rumors that he had died. They were so ecstatic when he showed up that they threw him a big party. They celebrated like the ten years that passed hadn't been piled on to their bodies. They laughed loudly as Juntaro recited to them everything that happened as if it was all a big joke, and Juntaro was drunk enough to think that it may as well have been. The day after, Juntaro was in bed all day with the worst hangover he'd ever had.

As he was getting his life back in order, he found it easier to catch up with what happened around the globe while he was stuck in the netherworld of Dokonimo. The internet had really taken off since he was gone and he found it easy to sit at a computer in the library and do research. It was a lot to take in. Japan had gone through six Prime Ministers, the new rail company had taken over transport in Tokyo in 2004, the economy was significantly improving, and America was still starting wars in the Middle East.

He tried doing research on where and what that Dokonimo place was, but all he could find was the occasional online post that mentioned it offhand. He would try contacting the people who made these posts, but none of them would ever respond. None of his friends or collaborators had heard of the place either. The Tokyo Metro offices treated him like a prank caller when he contacted them to ask about it. He tried to find the door in the Shinjuku station that Genzo had led them to that night, but where he would have sworn it was, there was only a wall.

He kept in contact with Kotono. She had a bit of a harder time adjusting. When she didn't come back, her company dismissed her and her apartment was rented to someone else after her family had taken her things out of it. Much of it was sold or given away. Her family had even held a funeral for her, certain that she was dead. Her mother and father were happy when she showed up at their door and invited her to stay with them until she was back on her feet. They quickly grew cold to her, though. They suspected she wasn't telling the truth about where she was the ten years she was missing. She moved out again as fast as she could.

One evening, Juntaro got a call from her.

"How have things been going?" she asked.

"It's been going well. I'm settled back in. How about you? Have you moved into your new place?"

"I have. Meguro is pretty different from Edogawa, but I like it here so far."

"You're a lot closer to Shinjuku too. We'll have to meet for a drink or something sometime."

"Of course! My new job is keeping me busy, but I'll get a hold of you when I have some free time."

"What are you doing now?"

"I'm actually working in the music industry now. Just as a receptionist for a talent agency, but I like it better than my old job."

"That's great!"

"I've got even more good news. I started writing poetry again, and I just got one accepted into a literary magazine!"

"Wow! That's great! Let me know when it's out. I'll need to get a copy and have you sign it."

Kotono laughed.

"Thank you!" she said. "I listened to that *Endless Humiliation* CD you sent me. It's really good, but it's so depressing. It reminds me of Masakatsu."

"Yeah, I recorded that during a very unhappy time in my life."

"Are you working on anything else?"

Juntaro thought for a moment.

"It's about time to get back to that, isn't it?"

"Yeah! The noisy stuff isn't my thing, but your music is great otherwise! You can't give up!"

"You're right. Thank you, Kotono. I'm going to get to work on something new right now."

"Okay! I'll talk to you later. I can't wait to hear your new album!"

Juntaro said goodbye and hung up. He looked over at his equipment. His turntable, his keyboards, his guitars, his pedals, his tape deck, and the computer he used to record. It had been a long time since he used any of it.

Ideas for music he wanted to make filled his head. They weren't happy sounds, but they were sounds he thought were worth being made.

ONE TWO THREE FOUR!

STORY IS OVER!

MUSIC IS BEGIN!

ACKNOWLEDGEMENTS
Thank you to the real life Juntaro Yamanouchi
for your unique music, all the inspiration that
you've given me, and for approving of this
novel. I hope you continue making music for
years to come.

Thank you to Alan Good and everyone at
Malarkey Books for publishing this book. I
couldn't ask for a better editor or press to
work with.

Thank you to Mark Wilson for your excellent
cover art.

Thank you to Michael Kazepis for doing the
typesetting and for the great work he's always
done for me.

Thank you to Cory for all your love and
support.

Thank you to my family for encouraging me.

And thank you, reader, for reading this
strange tale.

ABOUT THE AUTHOR

Ben Arzate lives in Des Moines, IA. He is
the author of the novels The Story of the Y
and Elaine, the short story collection The
Complete Idiot's Guide to Saying Goodbye, the
book of plays PLAYS/hauntologies, and the
poetry collections dr. sodom and mrs. gomorrah
and the sky is black and blue like a battered
child. He is a regular contributor to Cultured
Vultures and Babou 691. Find him online at
dripdropdripdropdripdrop.blogspot.com.

OTHER TITLES AVAILABLE OR FORTHCOMING FROM
MALARKEY BOOKS
--The Life of the Party Is Harder to Find Until
You're the Last One Around, Adrian Sobol
--Faith, Itoro Bassey
--Toadstones, Eric Williams
--White People on Vacation, Alex Miller
--Pontoon: volume 1, edited by Alan Good
--Don Bronco's (Working Title) Shell, Donald
Ryan
--Deliver Thy Pigs, Joey Hedger
--Your Favorite Poet, Leigh Chadwick
--It Came from the Swamp, edited by Joey R.
Poole
--Thunder from a Clear Blue Sky, Justin Bryant
--Guess What's Different, Susan Triemert
--Fearless, Benjamin Warner
--Man in a Cage, Patrick Nevins
--Un-ruined, Roger Vaillancourt

MalarkeyBooks.com

CPSIA information can be obtained
at www.ICGtesting.com
Printed in the USA
FSHW022318180122
87670FS